MUKI

The news of the Two's

By

YAMINAH ARMAND

"No, I do not want to be a big sister!" I screamed. "I thought you would be excited," replied mama. "Finally, you will have a little brother or sister to play with."

Mama had waited until after dinner to share her pregnancy news. Did she expect me to get excited? It did not work, I felt just the opposite. I wanted to vomit. Mama stared at me. She was not pleased. I could see it in her soft eyes.

I glanced over at Papa. He was calm and quiet. I was curious to know what he was thinking. "Muki, I am sorry you feel that way," Papa said at last, but having a sibling is not the end of the world." I knew Papa was right, but I am my parents' only child and I wanted it to stay that way.

The next day at school, I was feeling funny. I was not ready to be a big sister. "What would it be like having a little brother or sister?" I thought to myself.

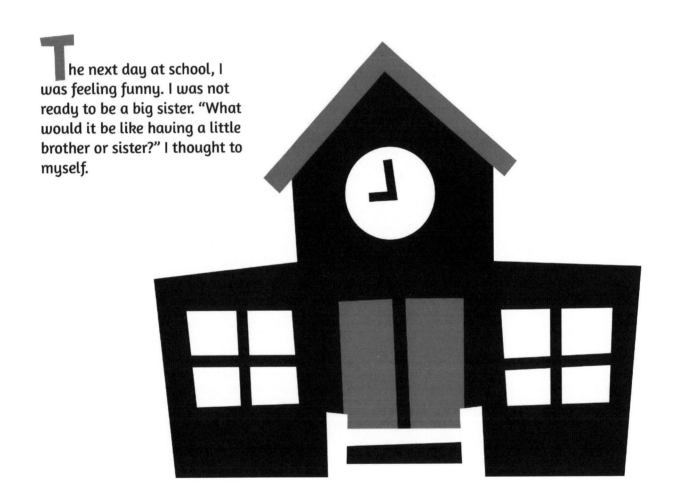

I did not want to share my feelings with my classmates and I was too shy to talk to Ms. Cecilia about it.

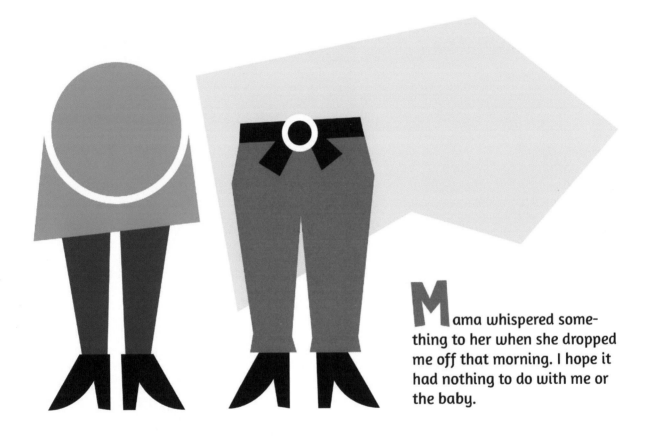

Mama whispered something to her when she dropped me off that morning. I hope it had nothing to do with me or the baby.

Suddenly, an idea popped into my head! I knew everyone in my class liked to play games, so I came up with a game of my own. One they would certainly be excited to play. I called my new game "How to Be a Big Sister or Brother."

In my sweetest voice, I asked: "Can I play a game with the class called "How to Be a Big Sister or Brother." Ms. Cecilia smiled and said: "What a wonderful idea, Muki." I beamed with joy. This was my chance to find out how to be a big sister.

I took my place in front of the class, as instructed by Ms. Cecilia, to give everyone the news and tell them the rules of the game. "Everyone, let's all sit in a circle to play a game! Each one of us will answer one question on how to be a big sister or brother. The person with the best idea is the winner. The class could barely hold back their excitement.

itting in the circle, Maria raised her hands and went first: "I do not have a little sister or brother, but I would like to have one. I think it would be fun," she said.

Elena went next: "My Papa and Mama would like to have a baby. I want it to be a girl so I can give it my old clothes and get new ones!" Ms. Cecilia's mouth twitched as if she was holding back a smile.

I gave her a worried glance. What if no one in the class had a sibling? I thought. Jànos stood up. He must have heard my thought.

"I have a baby sister and her name is Ana," he said. "She cries a lot and loves to drink milk." "After papa feeds her, she always burps."

BURP!

"When I do it, bu-uuurp, my Papa yells at me." The whole class, including Ms. Cecilia, burst into laughter. "She also farts and poops a lot." "Ewww," the class screamed in unison. "I wanted Jànos to stop. None of his ideas made me feel good about becoming a big sister at all."

And then it happened. Ms. Cecilia stood up. "Before I had a younger sibling, life was boring", she said. "However, that all changed when my brother was born." We all leaned in, eager to hear her story.

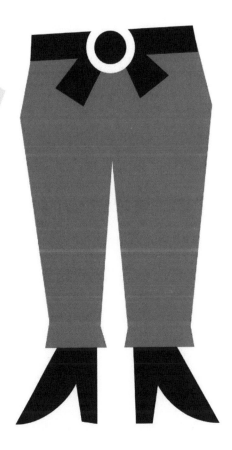

"**E**ven though he was younger, we had fun playing together. Going camping was also a lot of fun! Although, we would fight sometimes because my brother liked to tell on me. He would make me laugh so I could not stay mad at him for long!"

Ms. Cecilia continued, "Having a little sister or brother can be scary at first, but having a sibling, younger or older, is like having a life-long best friend. As you grow older, you will grow closer."

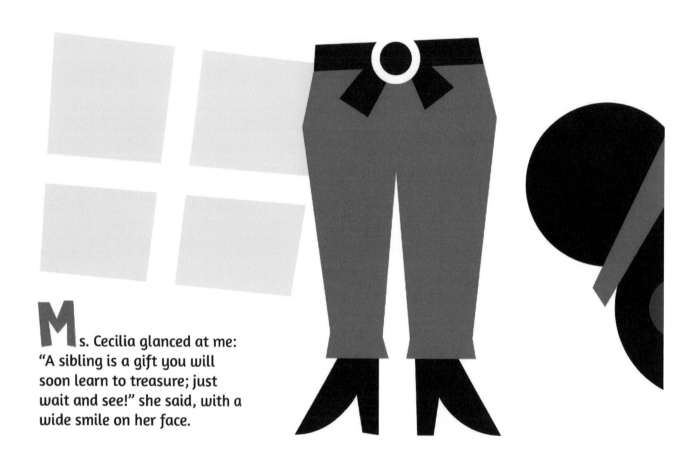

Ms. Cecilia glanced at me: "A sibling is a gift you will soon learn to treasure; just wait and see!" she said, with a wide smile on her face.

Instantly, I could feel my heart beating faster at the thought of a younger sibling. Maybe becoming a big sister will not be so bad after all. I have no idea what it will be like but I think I am willing to give it a try.

RINgg!

The bell rang. It was time to go home. Luckily, no one asked who the winner was but if I had to pick one, it would be Ms. Cecilia. I liked her story very much.

We all went back to our seats and organized our desks. We stood in line and followed Ms. Cecilia outside.

I looked around and spotted Papa in the crowd of parents. He waved at me to let me know he saw me too.
"Ms. Cecilia, my papa is here." Ms. Cecilia quickly checked to make sure he was there.

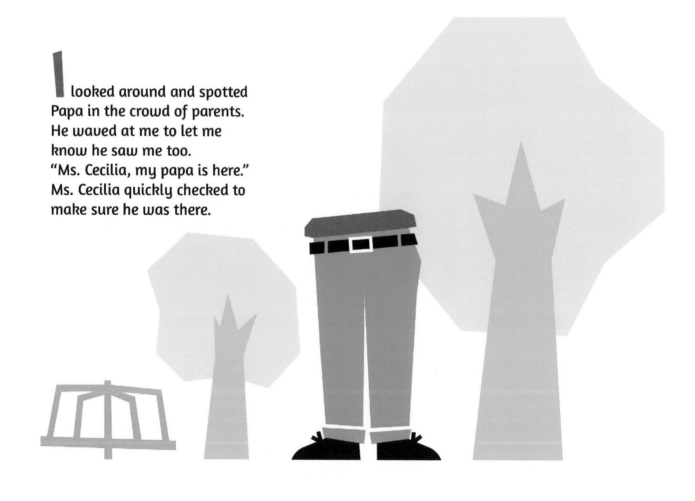

"**G**ood job today, Muki," she said. "I love your innovative spirit. Keep it up!" "Thank you Ms. Cecilia", I replied. We shook hands and said good-bye.

I could not wait to tell Papa about my day at school. "Guess what, Muki?" papa said, before I uttered a word. "Yes, papa?" I held my breath. Papa smiled softly, revealing the wrinkles around his eyes, "Mommy is expecting twins!"

TWINS?

"Twins?!" I screamed,
"Mommy's in big trouble now."
"I think we all are", Papa replied,
his smile turning into laughter.
We looked at each other and I
laughed along with him.

All I could think about on the way home was becoming a sister to not one baby, but two babies! I cannot wait to meet and play with the twins. It is going to be FUNTASTIC!

Printed in Great Britain
by Amazon